NCTE AWARD-WINNING POET

# I HEARD A BLUEBIRD SING

## CHILDREN SELECT THEIR FAVORITE POEMS BY

### AILEEN FISHER

### BERNICE E. CULLINAN, EDITOR

ILLUSTRATIONS BY
JENNIFER EMERY

WORDSONG
BOYDS MILLS PRESS

To boys and girls who love to read and wonder
—A. F.

To teachers who share their love of poetry with their students
—B. E. C.

To my parents, Ruth and Darrell Hall
—J. E.

Text copyright © 2002 by Aileen Fisher
Illustrations copyright © 2002 by Jennifer Emery
All rights reserved

Published by Wordsong
Boyds Mills Press, Inc.
A Highlights Company
815 Church Street
Honesdale, Pennsylvania 18431
Printed in China

Publisher Cataloging-in-Publication Data

Fisher, Aileen.
I heard a bluebird sing : children select their favorite poems / by Aileen Fisher ; Bernice E. Cullinan, editor ;
illustrations by Jennifer Emery. — 1st ed.
[64] p. : ill. ; cm.
At head of title: NCTE Award-Winning Poet.
Includes index.
Summary: Young readers select their favorite poems of Aileen Fisher, winner of the National Council of
Teachers of English Award for Poetry for Children.
Note: Introduction created from previously published writings of Aileen Fisher included.
ISBN 1-56397-191-7
1. Children's poetry, American. (1. Poetry.) I. Cullinan, Bernice E. II. Emery, Jennifer, ill. III. Title.
811.54 21 2002 CIP AC
2001098609

First edition, 2002
The text of this book is set in 15-point Cochin.

Visit our Web site at www.boydsmillspress.com.

10 9 8 7 6 5 4 3 2 1

Portrait of Aileen Fisher by Marc Nadel
Permissions can be found on page 61.

# CONTENTS

The National Council of Teachers of English
Award for Poetry for Children is presented once every three
years to a poet for a distinguished body of work sustained
over a period of time and honors the memory of
Jonathan Paul Cullinan,
a child who loved books.

# PREFACE

I wanted to publish a companion volume to *A Jar of Tiny Stars: Poems by NCTE Award-Winning Poets* that focused on Aileen Fisher's poems, since she was an early recipient of the National Council of Teachers of English Award for Poetry for Children. It was fun to read every possible Aileen Fisher poem I could locate — some out of print, some recently written, some funny, and all with vivid images. A small panel of teachers helped me to select eighty poems we thought children would like. We grouped these into four sets of twenty poems with a variety of topics and appeal. We sent the sets of poems to teachers and librarians across the United States, who shared them with children.

During class, some teachers asked, "What did you notice about Aileen Fisher's poetry?" This is what some of the students said:

"She never forces her rhyme."

"She likes stuff that children like."

"She sometimes talks in children's voices."

"She must spend a lot of time on poetry because they always turn out good."

"She wonders a lot."

"She puts herself in it."

"She puts questions in her poems."

"She builds suspense in her poems."

"Her poetry is very powerful and fantastic."

The children then voted for their top ten favorite poems. All votes were tabulated. The top ten poems from each set are included in this book. Names of participating teachers and librarians and their schools are listed on the acknowledgment page.

BERNICE E. CULLINAN
Professor, New York University
Editor in chief, Wordsong

# ACKNOWLEDGMENTS

A special thanks goes to the following teachers and librarians:

Marty Abbondandelo, Glenwood Landing School, Glen Head, New York

Barbara Allgood, Riverhill School, Florence, Alabama

Gerry Bain-Ryder, Glenwood Landing School, Glen Head, New York

Jocelyn Balaban, The Mirman School, Los Angeles, California

Alisa Barbera, Monsey Elementary School, Monsey, New York

Linda Baylor, Leacock Elementary School, Gordonville, Pennsylvania

Ann Blackburn, Lake Highland Preparatory School, Orlando, Florida

Dale Bowling, Riverhill School, Florence, Alabama

Rick Boyle, St. Joseph School, Seattle, Washington

Elaine Bradshaw, Lake Highland Preparatory School, Orlando, Florida

Sandra Brand, Academy Elementary School, Madison, Connecticut

Kim Bush, Lake Highland Preparatory School, Orlando, Florida

Karen Carter, Riverhill School, Florence, Alabama

Michelle Choate, Madison Cross Roads School, Toney, Alabama

Susan Coop, Lake Highland Preparatory School, Orlando, Florida

Barbara Cooper, Glenwood Landing School, Glen Head, New York

Kathy Copenhaver, Logan Public Schools, Logan, Utah

Julia Candace Corliss, The Mirman School, Los Angeles, California

Carol Croland, Echo Horizon School, Culver City, California

Patricia Cugno, Glenwood Landing School, Glen Head, New York

Laurie Ann Cusick, Horace Mann Foreign Language Magnet School, Wichita, Kansas

Penny D'Alessandro, Leacock Elementary School, Gordonville, Pennsylvania

Judy Davis, Manhattan New School, New York, New York

Barbara Deery, Lake Highland Preparatory School, Orlando, Florida

Linda Chronister Depro, Leacock Elementary School, Gordonville, Pennsylvania

Margaret M. DeSimone, Memorial School, Burlington, Massachusetts

Linda Flynn, Bluff Ridge Elementary School, Syracuse, Utah

Mary Jo Fresch, Dublin Public Schools, Dublin, Ohio

Lee Galda, Minneapolis Public Schools, Minneapolis, Minnesota

Iris Gandler, Munsey Park Elementary School, Manhasset, New York

Rudy Gebig, Munsey Park Elementary School, Manhasset, New York

Bob Giannuzzi, Glenwood Landing School, Glen Head, New York

Alice Giovanniello, Memorial School, Burlington, Massachusetts

Sherry Goubeaux, Upper Arlington Public Schools, Upper Arlington, Ohio

Janet Helmer, Clairbourn School, San Gabriel, California

Gloria Hidalgo, Phoenix Public Schools, Phoenix, Arizona

Joie Hinden, Manhasset High School, Manhasset, New York

Helen Hoofer, Lewis Open Magnet School, Wichita, Kansas

Diedre Humphrey, Glenwood Landing School, Glen Head, New York

Michelle Ingraham, Lake Highland Preparatory School, Orlando, Florida

Diane Ingvarsson, Memorial School, Burlington, Massachusetts

Racquel Kislinger, Polytechnic School, Pasadena, California

Anita Knight, Clairbourn School, San Gabriel, California

Zeva La Horgue, Polytechnic School, Pasadena, California

Jacqueline Lane, Wichita Public Schools, Wichita, Kansas

Stephanie Langston, Lake Highland Preparatory School, Orlando, Florida

Lynn Leslie, Glenwood Landing School, Glen Head, New York

Judith Mack, Memorial School, Burlington, Massachusetts

Donnie Mai, Taft Elementary School, Orange, California

Mary G. Maloney, Munsey Park Elementary School, Manhasset, New York

Johanna Markworth, Lewiston Elementary School, Logan, Utah

Susan A. Mathis, Brookwood Elementary School, Sandy, Utah

Donna McAlpin, Riverhill School, Florence, Alabama

Monica McCoun, Taft Elementary School, Orange, California

Nancy McIntosh, Lake Highland Preparatory School, Orlando, Florida

Jane Medina, Taft Elementary School, Orange, California

Anita Melnick, Echo Horizon School, Culver City, California

Judy Merker, Taft Elementary School, Orange, California

Brooks C. Mills, Lake Highland Preparatory School, Orlando, Florida

Debbie Minicozzi, Glenwood Landing School, Glen Head, New York

Susan Moore-Patel, Glenwood Landing School, Glen Head, New York

Cathi Ostrom, Chapala Elementary School, Santa Barbara, California

Ramona Otto, The Mirman School, Los Angeles, California

Margaret Lynn Owens, Wildwood Elementary School, Wildwood, Missouri

Nancy Peet, Munsey Park Elementary School, Manhasset, New York

Rebecca Pierce, Lake Highland Preparatory School, Orlando, Florida

Susan Pringle, Lake Highland Preparatory School, Orlando, Florida

Christine Purpura, Glenwood Landing School, Glen Head, New York

Mai Ramerez, Glenwood Landing School, Glen Head, New York

Cindy Read, College Hill School, Wichita, Kansas

Donna Reihing, Glenwood Landing School, Glen Head, New York

Audrey Risden, Polytechnic School, Pasadena, California

Bridget Rooney, Glenwood Landing School, Glen Head, New York

Nancy Roser, Austin Public Schools, Austin, Texas

Joelle Ross, Lake Highland Preparatory School, Orlando, Florida

Sally Rubin, Memorial School, Burlington, Massachusetts

Sara Ruth, Leacock Elementary School, Gordonville, Pennsylvania

Jenny Ryan, Echo Horizon School, Culver City, California

Joanne Hindley Salch, Manhattan New School, New York, New York

Tracy Salviolo, Glenwood Landing School, Glen Head, New York

Marilyn Scala, Brooklyn Public Schools, Brooklyn, New York

Ginnie Schroder, Lakeland Public Schools, Lakeland, New York

Carol Shearer, Leacock Elementary School, Gordonville, Pennsylvania

Jane Shimotsu, The Mirman School, Los Angeles, California

Larry Shurr, Leacock Elementary School, Gordonville, Pennsylvania

Marion G. Siefert, Fairmount School, St. Peters, Missouri

Susan Sigle, John Marshall Middle School, Wichita, Kansas

Alex Slobodskoy, Glenwood Landing School, Glen Head, New York

Marcy Smith, Echo Horizon School, Culver City, California

Cathi Speake, Santa Barbara Junior High, Santa Barbara, California

Leanne Statland, The Mirman School, Los Angeles, California

Linda Stowitts, Polytechnic School, Pasadena, California

Julie Taylor, Salt Lake City Public Schools, Salt Lake City, Utah

Barbara Thomas, Glendale Public Schools, Glendale, Arizona

Marci Vogel, Echo Horizon School, Culver City, California

Pam Wable, Fairmount School, St. Peters, Missouri

Jacqueline Wachsman, Hewlett Public Schools, Hewlett, New York

Jan Walker, Lake Highland Preparatory School, Orlando, Florida

Judy Walker, Lake Highland Preparatory School, Orlando, Florida

Shanna Wellons, Lake Highland Preparatory School, Orlando, Florida

Aileen Wheaton, Bailey Elementary School, Dublin, Ohio

Sue Wickey, Glenwood Landing School, Glen Head, New York

Nance Wilson, Lake Highland Preparatory School, Orlando, Florida

Susan Wilson, Polytechnic School, Pasadena, California

Dorothy Wooddell, Polytechnic School, Pasadena, California

Deborah Wooten, Glenwood Landing School, Glen Head, New York

Denise Wreede, Clairbourn School, San Gabriel, California

# INTRODUCTION

In an article published in *Highlights for Children* magazine a number of years ago, Aileen Fisher shared her thoughts with readers about writing. Excerpts from her article and interviews appear below and at the beginning of each section of this book.

How does a writer go about becoming a writer? My answer is very brief: read, read, read. See how different writers use words to make things happen or to point up a thought or feeling. Then write down some of your own words and hide them away for a while. When you take them out, read them aloud. How do you think they sound? In the meantime, keep reading!

Where does the inspiration come from? From all around you. From the people you know, the sights you see, the things you do and remember, and particularly from the way you feel. Writers aren't all inspired by the same things. Some of them turn to nature, some of them love the city with its beehives of lighted windows, some of them live in a world of fancies. Open yourself to whatever means the most to you, and ideas will flow in. And in the meantime, keep reading.

How do you get started? By doing, by practicing . . . just as you learn to throw a Frisbee or play a musical instrument. You don't start out being a writer any more than you start out being a violinist. You build up to it. You practice patiently. It usually takes a while before a writer can get something published. But in the meantime you can make progress by reading what other writers have written.

As far as my own writing is concerned, I was no child prodigy by any means. I occasionally thought up verses when I was in grade school. And I contributed to the school column in the weekly newspaper when I was in high school. But it wasn't until my senior year in college that I began seriously hoping I might become a writer. And what do you think I turned to for inspiration? My childhood in the Upper Peninsula of Michigan. I have been turning to it ever since!

Ideas for poems lie all around us, in the everyday things we see and do and think and feel and remember, as well as in unusual sights and happenings. In the city as well as in the country, poems are waiting to be discovered, yours for the taking. Who knows . . . perhaps you are living a poem right now which some day you will put down on paper.

# Family and Friends

I had a lucky childhood. When I was five years old, my father was advised by the doctor to give up his business and move to the country where life would be less strenuous. And so the fall I entered the first grade we were living in a big white house on the bank above a river, two miles from town. I couldn't imagine a better place to live.

My father's "less strenuous life" gave me a wonderfully varied background. We always had a big garden, a wheat field and a hayfield, and farm animals to look after. I remember standing and watching the hayfield on a windy day:

> *I like to see the wind*
> *go racing through the hay:*
> *it's just like a green fire*
> *galloping away.*
> *It's a field full of green flames*
> *licking at the hill.*
> *And then it's just a hayfield*
> *. . . when the wind is still.*

On my eighth birthday a sister was born. I took immediate charge of her because she was, after all, my birthday present.

# GROWING

When I ask Mother
she doesn't really know:
"What's inside of me
making me grow?"

So I ask Father
who doesn't grow a bit:
"What's inside of YOU
making you quit?"

And Father says, "Hmmm . . .
I'm — busy — now, son . . ."
So I STILL don't know
how growing is done.

# PLANS

When I make Plans
that are grand and vast,
even more grand than
the time-before-last,
how can my mother
say "NO!" so fast?

# IF I WERE MY MOTHER

If I were my mother
I rarely would make
omelet, or parsnips,
or spinach, or steak,
or carrots, or onions—
I'd much rather bake
doughnuts and pudding
and dumplings and cake.

I'd not take the trouble
to cut up a lot
of turnips—instead I'd
make jam in a pot,
and fritters, and cookies,
and pies piping hot . . .
if I were my mother.
Too bad that I'm not!

# FAIRY TALE

I read in a book of a daughter who
made three wishes that all came true.

So I wished my mother would call, "Come, quick,
there's a spoon and a frosting bowl to lick."

And I wished my mother would call, "Make haste!
Here's a nice hot cookie for you to taste."

And I wished my mother would say, "Why, ye-es,
it's foolish to practice your scales, I guess."

I wished, and wished—but I must admit
it didn't work out like the book a BIT.

# BIRTHDAY

The next best thing to Christmas,
the next best day to prize
is a birthday, when you're special
in everybody's eyes.

The next best thing to Christmas
if it's summer, spring, or fall,
is a birthday with a party
and a birthday cake and all.

# BIRTHDAY PRESENT

No, not something
to read, or eat,
but something
with race-away, chase-away feet.

No, not something
to ride, or wear,
but something
with rumpledy, frumpledy hair.

No, not something
inside a bag,
but something
with something outside to wag . . .

That's what I want,
the best thing yet,
and that's what I hope,
hope, hope I'll get.

# CLIMBING

The trunk of a tree
is the road for me
on a sunny summer day.

Up the bark
that is brown and dark
through tunnels of leaves that sway
and tickle my knees
in the trembly breeze,
that's where I make my way.

    Leaves in my face
    and twigs in my hair
    in a squeeze of a place,
    but I don't care!

*Some* people talk
of a summer walk
through clover and weeds and hay.

*Some* people stride
where the hills are wide
and the rocks are speckled gray.

But the trunk of a tree
is the road for me
on a sunny summer day.

# HIDEOUT

They looked for me
and from my nook
inside the oak
I watched them look.

Through little slits
between the leaves
I saw their looking
legs and sleeves.

They would have looked
all over town
except —
I threw some acorns down.

# NEW NEIGHBORS

When Smiths packed up
and moved away,
and Judy was gone,
I cried all day.

I knew I'd *never*
like anyone
as much as Judy
or have such fun.

Then Browns moved in
with a silky cat
and a dog with puppies.
Imagine that!

And a girl named Becky . . .
and I forgot
all about missing
Judy a lot.

# STAYING OVERNIGHT

For dinner at Donna's
we had green peas.
At home I'm not very fond of these.
But I ate them all
'cause company should.
And what do you think?
They tasted good.

For breakfast at Donna's
we had oatmeal.
I've never been fond of its taste or feel.
But there wasn't a choice
of oatmeal OR . . .
And what do you think?
I asked for more.

# Pets

When I was a child we always had cats and dogs to play with. I have written many verses about them. I now live in Boulder, Colorado, at the edge of town on a dead-end street, close to Flagstaff Mountain. The highlight of each day is a walk with my dog and a friend and her dog on one of the many trails nearby. This keeps me in touch with the weather, the wildlife, and the wonderful scenery in every direction.

## MY PUPPY

It's funny
my puppy
knows just how I feel:

When I'm happy
he's yappy
and squirms like an eel.

When I'm grumpy
he's slumpy
and stays at my heel.

It's funny
my puppy
knows such a great deal.

## MY DOG GINGER

He's reddish
and brownish,
like gingersnap spice.

He's eager
and clownish
and silky and nice.

And when it comes
to kissing me
when he is full
of missing me,
he never stops
at only once
or even only twice.

# A PONY

Wish I had a pony
who would nuzzle, nuzzle, nuzzle
with his silky-satin muzzle.

Wish I had a pony
I could straddle, straddle, straddle,
so I wouldn't need a saddle.

Wish I had a white one,
a just-the-proper-height one.

Wish I had a red one,
a star-upon-his-head one.

Wish I had a brown one,
a trotting-up-and-down one.

Wish I had a pony
with a name like Tuck or Tony
who was plump instead of bony
(though a bony one would do) . . .

Wish it didn't take so long
for wishes to come true.

# MY CAT

My cat rubs my leg
and starts to purr
with a soft little rumble,
a soft little whirr,
as if she had motors
inside of her.

I say, "Nice kitty,"
and stroke her fur,
and though she can't talk
and I can't purr,
she understands me,
and I do her.

# CAT BATH

After she eats,
my purry friend
washes herself
from end to end.

Washes her face,
her ears, her paws,
washes the pink
between her claws.

I watch and think
it's better by far
to splash in a tub
with soap in a bar

And washcloth in hand
and towel on the rung
than to have to do all
that work BY TONGUE.

# Clever Creatures

We had horses that knew how to twitch their skins to scare off the flies, and cows that knew how to turn green grass into white milk and yellow cream, and chickens that were expert at making eggs. It was my job to gather eggs each evening.

*I wonder how*
*an egg's begun.*
*The yolk*
*is yellow as the sun.*
*The color of the white*
*is . . . none.*
*You'd think the yolk*
*and white would run*
*before the shell*
*was ever done . . .*
*But hens don't lay*
*a scrambled one!*

# *KNOWING*

Nobody teaches
a bird to sing
or a frog to croak
as soon as it's spring.

Nobody teaches
a bee to make honey
or shows how-to-hop
to a new little bunny.

Nobody teaches
a spider to spin . . .
How do they know
what to do to **BEGIN?**

## TIGHTROPE WALKER

If I were the spider
walking there
on a thread of silk
in a world of air,

Above all blue,
and beneath all brown,
I'd get so dizzy
I'd fall right down.

# BUSY SUMMER

Bees
make wax and honey,

Spiders,
webs of silk.

Wasps
make paper houses.

Cows
make cream and milk.

Dandelions
make pollen
for the bees to take.

Wish that I
had something
I knew how to make.

# UPSIDE DOWN

It's funny how beetles
and creatures like that
can walk upside down
as well as walk flat.

They crawl on a ceiling
and climb on a wall
without any practice
or trouble at all,

While *I* have been trying
for a year (maybe more)
and still I can't stand
with my head on the floor.

# TWICE BORN

For moths and butterflies, it's nice:
they get born once, they get born twice.

They get born first from tiny eggs
as caterpillars having legs.

They get born next from silk cocoons,
with *wings*, on summer afternoons.

If *I* should get a second try,
I'd like to grow some wings, and fly.

# BUTTERFLY WINGS

How would it be
on a day in June
to open your eyes
in a dark cocoon,

And soften one end
and crawl outside,
and find you had wings
to open wide,

And find you could fly
to a bush or tree
or float on the air
like a boat at sea . . .

How would it BE?

## BABY CHICK

Peck, peck, peck
on the warm brown egg.
Out comes a neck!
Out comes a leg!

How does a chick,
who's not been about,
discover the trick
of how to get out?

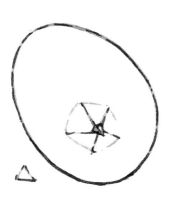

# SNAIL'S PACE

Maybe it's so
that snails are slow:
they trudge along and tarry.

But isn't it true
you'd slow up, too,
if you had a house to carry?

# Wild Ones

My house is well back from the street. Skunks and raccoons live nearby, and last year I even found a baby porcupine in my yard. In the winter, deer come right down into this end of town, and I often see groups of them on the side of Flagstaff Mountain. I must say city living could be a lot worse!

# THE FURRY ONES

I like
the furry ones—
the waggy ones
the purry ones
the hoppy ones
that hurry,

The glossy ones
the saucy ones
the sleepy ones
the leapy ones
the mousy ones
that scurry,

The snuggly ones
the hug-ly ones
the never, never
ugly ones . . .
all soft
and warm
and furry.

## AT NIGHT

In the still dark depths
of the pines and birches,
day-birds sleep
on their hidden perches.

A woodchuck curls
in his burrow bed,
a squirrel in his leaf-nest
overhead.

And down in his tunnel
a chippy is dozing,
comfy and quiet
and never supposing
that out in the starlight
a doe and a fawn
are picking his daisies
and mowing his lawn!

# MOUSE DINNER

A mouse doesn't dine
on potatoes and beef . . .
he nibbles the seeds
from a pod or a sheaf.

He catches a beetle
and then gives a brief
little wipe of his mouth
on a napkin of leaf.

# BLUEBIRD

In the woods a piece of sky
fell down, a piece of blue.
"It must have come from very high,"
I said. "It looks so new."

It landed on a leafy tree
and there it seemed to cling,
and when I squinted up to see,
I saw it had a *wing*,
and then a *head*, and suddenly
I heard a bluebird sing!

# THE HAWK

Instead of using his wings to fly
the hawk just waits on a hill of sky
till a frisky wind that blows from town
swishes him up and swoops him down.

Instead of using a pine or birch
he makes a frollicking wind his perch,
and tilts his wings till away he glides
to the roof of the sky and down its sides.

Wish *I* knew how to get such tides!

# THE SPARROW

I found a speckled sparrow
between the showers of rain.

He thought the window wasn't there
and flew against the pane.

I picked him up and held him.
He didn't stir at all.

I hardly felt him in my hand,
he was so soft and small.

I held him like a flower
upon my open palm.

I saw an eyelid quiver,
though he lay still and calm.

And then . . . before I knew it
I stood alone, aghast:

I never thought a bird so limp
could fly away so fast!

# WHEN IT COMES TO BUGS

I like crawlers,
I like creepers,
hoppers, jumpers,
fliers, leapers,
walkers, stalkers,
chirpers, peepers . . .

I wonder why
my mother thinks
that finders can't be keepers?

# A CRICKET

In a matchbox
is a cricket
with a patent-leather shine.
It's at Peter's,
and he's printed
MISTER CRICKET on a sign.

In a fruit jar
that is open,
with a leaf on which to dine,
is a cricket
that is Kathy's
and she thinks it's very fine.

Nothing's gayer
than a cricket!
Nothing's louder after nine!
But my mother
thinks a *thicket*
is the nicest place for mine.

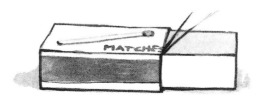

# *FEET*

Feet of snails
are only one.
Birds grow two
to hop and run.
Dogs and cats
and cows grow four.
Ants and beetles
add two more.
Spiders run around
on eight,
which may seem
a lot, but wait —
Centipedes
have more than *thirty*
feet to wash
when they get dirty.

# BEARS

I wouldn't be a bear
for several reasons.

My main objection
has to do with seasons:

For one thing, I'd not like
hot fur in summer,

But then, I think the winters
would be dumber. . . .

Imagine! curling up where
there's no heating

And sleeping months and months
and never eating.

NEVER EATING!

# Weather and Seasons

W<sup></sup>e lived close to weather in the country. My brother and I walked back and forth to school no matter how cold or wet or warm it was. We rarely missed a day.

Spring was always filled with "firsts"—the first spring beauties in the woods near the culvert, the first violets and cowslips along the river, the first warm-enough day to go barefoot. All around us we found evidences that "only *icicles* weep tears when spring appears, when spring appears."

Summer brought wild berries to pick (and potato bugs) and camping at the lake where we swam by day and chased fireflies at dusk. And summer meant riding on top of a load of hay, and watching the threshers, and going on picnics.

Then September came . . . and school again, and wearing shoes again, and watching maple leaves turn red and poplar leaves turn yellow. I always felt a little sad about fall . . .

> *The last of October*
> *the birds have all flown,*
> *the screens are in the attic,*
> *the sandpile's alone.*
> *Everything is put away*
> *before it starts to snow . . .*
> *I wonder if the ladybugs*
> *have any place to go?*

But the temporary sadness of fall soon vanished. In northern Michigan, winter comes early and stays late, and for us children winter was a great time of year. Out came skis and sleds and skates. Up went snow forts and snowmen and snowhouses.

> *It's snowing! It's snowing!*
> *The piles of white are growing,*
> *and when we hold our mittens out*
> *we gather falling stars.*

(I can still smell the steamy wetness of mittens drying on the warming oven of the kitchen range.)

# *WEATHER*

Weather is full
of the nicest sounds:
it sings
and rustles
and pings
and pounds
and hums
and tinkles
and strums
and twangs
and whishes
and sprinkles
and splishes
and bangs
and mumbles
and grumbles
and rumbles
and flashes
and CRASHES.

# DEER MOUSE

Who tells the little deer mouse
when summer goes away
that she should fix a cozy place,
a comfy place to stay,
and fill her cupboard shelves with seeds
from berries, weeds, and hay?

Who tells the little deer mouse
before the year is old
that she should wear a warmer coat
to shield her from the cold?
I'm glad that *someone* tells her
and she does as she is told.

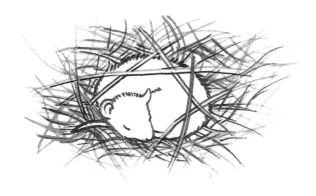

# AUTUMN CONCERT

In the evening
in the thickets

There are orchestras
of crickets,

And you never
need buy *tickets*

To hear concerts
by the crickets.

## IN THE SNOW OR SUN

I wear outer clothes and inner,
sometimes thicker, sometimes thinner.

When the yellow days turn grayer
I wear layer after layer,
with a parka or a sweater,
or a slicker when it's wetter.

But a dog or cat or camel
or some other kind of mammal
like a woodchuck or a rabbit
has a less expensive habit,
wearing all its clothes *in one*
in the rain or snow or sun.

# SNOWBALL WIND

The wind was throwing snowballs.
It plucked them from the trees
and tossed them all around the woods
as boldly as you please.

I ducked beneath the spruces
which didn't help a speck;
the wind kept throwing snowballs
and threw one down my neck.

## MERRY CHRISTMAS

I saw on the snow
when I tried my skis
the track of a mouse
beside some trees.

Before he tunneled
to reach his house
he wrote "Merry Christmas"
in white, in mouse.

# *VALENTINES*

I gave a hundred Valentines.
A hundred, did I say?
I gave a *thousand* Valentines
one cold and wintry day.

I didn't put my name on them
or any other words,
because my Valentines were seeds
for February birds.

# THE SPINNING EARTH

The earth, they say,
spins round and round.
It doesn't look it
from the ground,
and never makes
a spinning sound.

And water never
swirls and swishes
from oceans full
of dizzy fishes,
and shelves don't lose
their pans and dishes.

And houses don't go whirling by,
or puppies swirl around the sky,
or robins spin instead of fly.

It may be true
what people say
about our spinning
night and day . . .
but I keep wondering
        anyway.

# PERMISSIONS

The poems in this book were previously published in the books listed below. All poems are reprinted by permission of Marian Reiner for the author.

"Weather," "My Cat," "The Spinning Earth," "Cat Bath," "Baby Chick," "Snail's Pace," "Knowing," "My Puppy," "Bears," "Valentines," "Merry Christmas," and "Butterfly Wings" from *Always Wondering*, illustrated by Joan Sandin, published by HarperCollins. Copyright © 1991 by Aileen Fisher.

"Mouse Dinner," "Twice Born," "Autumn Concert," and "In the Snow or Sun" from *Out in the Dark and Daylight*, illustrated by Gail Owens, published by Harper & Row (HarperCollins). Copyright © 1980 by Aileen Fisher.

"Bluebird," "Climbing," "Hideout," "Snowball Wind," and "Busy Summer" from *In the Woods, In the Meadow, In the Sky*, illustrated by Margot Tomes, published by Charles Scribner's Sons. Copyright © 1965 by Aileen Fisher. Copyright renewed 1993 by Aileen Fisher.

"Plans," "If I Were My Mother," "New Neighbors," "Growing," "Tightrope Walker," "Fairy Tale," "Birthday," "Staying Overnight," and "My Dog Ginger" from *In One Door and Out the Other*, illustrated by Lillian Hoban, published by Thomas Y. Crowell (HarperCollins). Copyright © 1969 by Aileen Fisher. Copyright renewed 1997 by Aileen Fisher.

"When It Comes to Bugs" and "Upside Down" from *When It Comes to Bugs*, illustrated by Chris and Bruce Degen, published by Harper & Row (HarperCollins). Copyright © 1986 by Aileen Fisher.

"The Furry Ones," "A Pony," "The Sparrow," and "The Hawk" from *Feathered Ones and Furry*, illustrated by Eric Carle, published by Thomas Y. Crowell (HarperCollins). Copyright © 1971 by Aileen Fisher. Copyright renewed 1999 by Aileen Fisher.

"Feet," "A Cricket," "Birthday Present," "At Night," and "Deer Mouse" from *Cricket in a Thicket*, illustrated by Feodor Rojankovsky, published by Charles Scribner's Sons. Copyright © 1963 by Aileen Fisher. Copyright renewed 1991 by Aileen Fisher.

# SELECTED WORKS BY AILEEN FISHER

*The Coffee-Pot Face*, illustrated by the author. New York: Junior Literary Guild and Robert M. McBride & Co., 1933.

*Inside a Little House*, illustrated by the author. New York: Robert M. McBride & Co., 1938.

*That's Why*, illustrated by the author. New York: T. Nelson & Sons, 1946.

*Up the Windy Hill: Book of Merry Verse with Silhouettes*, illustrated by the author. New York: Abelard Press, 1953.

*Runny Days, Sunny Days: Merry Verses*, illustrated by the author. New York: Abelard-Schuman, 1958.

*Going Barefoot*, illustrated by Adrienne Adams. New York: Thomas Y. Crowell, 1960.

*Where Does Everyone Go?*, illustrated by Adrienne Adams. New York, Thomas Y. Crowell, 1961.

*I Wonder How, I Wonder Why*, illustrated by Carol Barker. New York: Abelard-Schuman, 1962.

*Like Nothing at All*, illustrated by Leonard Weisgard. New York: Thomas Y. Crowell, 1962.

*I Like Weather*, illustrated by Janina Domanska. New York: Thomas Y. Crowell, 1963.

*Cricket in a Thicket*, illustrated by Feodor Rojankovsky. New York: Charles Scribner's Sons, 1963.

*Listen, Rabbit*, illustrated by Symeon Shimin. New York: Thomas Y. Crowell, 1964.

*In the Middle of the Night*, illustrated by Adrienne Adams. Thomas Y. Crowell, 1965.

*In the Woods, In the Meadow, In the Sky*, illustrated by Margot Tomes. New York: Charles Scribner's Sons, 1965.

*Best Little House*, illustrated by Arnold Spilka. New York: Thomas Y. Crowell, 1966.

*Skip Around the Year*, illustrated by Gioia Fiammenghi. New York: Thomas Y. Crowell, 1967.

*My Mother and I*, illustrated by Kazue Mizumura. New York: Thomas Y. Crowell, 1967.

*Up, Up the Mountain*, illustrated by Gilbert Riswold. New York: Thomas Y. Crowell, 1968.

*We Went Looking*, illustrated by Marie Angel. New York: Thomas Y. Crowell, 1968.

*Clean as a Whistle*, illustrated by Ben Shecter. New York: Thomas Y. Crowell, 1969.

*In One Door and Out the Other: A Book of Poems*, illustrated by Lillian Hoban. New York: Thomas Y. Crowell, 1969.

*Sing, Little Mouse*, illustrated by Symeon Shimin. New York: Thomas Y. Crowell, 1969.

*But Ostriches . . .* , illustrated by Peter Parnall. New York: Thomas Y. Crowell, 1970.

*Feathered Ones and Furry*, illustrated by Eric Carle. New York: Thomas Y. Crowell, 1971.

*Do Bears Have Mothers Too?*, illustrated by Eric Carle. New York: Thomas Y. Crowell, 1973.

*My Cat Has Eyes of Sapphire Blue*, illustrated by Marie Angel. New York: Thomas Y. Crowell, 1973.

*Once We Went on a Picnic*, illustrated by Tony Chen. New York: Thomas Y. Crowell, 1975.

*I Stood upon a Mountain*, illustrated by Blair Lent. New York: Thomas Y. Crowell, 1979.

*Anybody Home?*, illustrated by Susan Bonners. New York: Thomas Y. Crowell, 1980.

*Out in the Dark and Daylight*, illustrated by Gail Owens. New York: Harper & Row, 1980.

*Rabbits, Rabbits*, illustrated by Gail Niemann. New York: Harper & Row, 1983.

*In Summer* (with Jane Belk Moncure), illustrated by Marie-Claude Monchaux. Elgin, Illinois: Child's World, 1985.

*When It Comes to Bugs*, illustrated by Chris and Bruce Degen. New York, Harper & Row, 1986.

*The House of a Mouse*, illustrated by Joan Sandin. New York: Harper & Row, 1988.

*Always Wondering*, illustrated by Joan Sandin. New York: HarperCollins, 1991.

*Sing of the Earth and Sky: Poems about Our Planet and the Wonders Beyond*, illustrated by Karmen Thompson. Honesdale, Pennsylvania: Wordsong/Boyds Mills Press, 2001.

# INDEX
## by *Title* and First Line